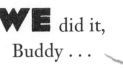

· CHAPTER 1 ·
EAR WE GO

I regret it . . .
I regret it . . .

I feel like we should say something . . .

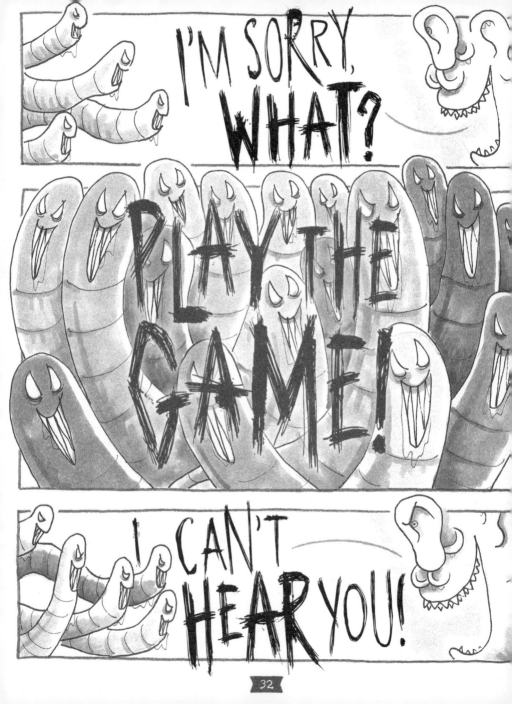

ALL YOU HAVE to DO IS CROSS THE ARENA AND GET to THE NEXT DOORWAY. SEE? IT'S RIGHT THERE! EASY! AND IF YOU SUCCEED...

ARE YOU
READY?

This is *probably*
not as easy as he's
making it sound . . .

EXCELLENT!

OHHH, ONE MORE THING!

MEET OUR MOST RECENT STAR PLAYERS!

Oh no . . .

PIRANHA!
ARE YOU OK?!

IT'S NOT
GOOD,
CHICO!

YOU GUYS
NEED TO
BLOCK YOUR . . .

· CHAPTER 2 ·
MILTON

WE'RE COMING UP ON **EARTH!**

Milt?

You're **ONE OF THE OTHERS?!**

What do you mean,
you're one of The Others . . . ?

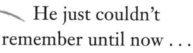

Well, he has been gone a LOOOOOONG time . . .

OK.
Someone needs to
TELL US WHAT'S GOING ON!

mrrff!

But HOW can Milt
be one of The Others?
Aren't The Others
missing pieces of
THE ONE?

That's right, beautiful spider.

But Milt is from
**60 MILLION
YEARS AGO!**
We **RANDOMLY**
picked him up in a
**TIME-TRAVEL
ACCIDENT.**
It was a total MISHAP!

that it **WASN'T** an accident?

What? Someone **DELIBERATELY** sent us MILLIONS OF YEARS BACK IN TIME to collect **THIS EXACT DINOSAUR?!**

Stranger things have happened!

No.
They haven't.

Agreed.
They really haven't.
Ever.
In history.

But even if someone **DID** deliberately
send us back through time,
WHY would one of The Others be hidden
ALL THE WAY BACK
in ancient history anyway?!
It doesn't make any sense!

... with a **DINOSAUR** who **ATE ME** to give himself the power to turn a **CHAIN SAW GUY** into a **LITTLE SPOON GUY,** and now that **SAME DINOSAUR** is telling us ...

he belongs with this **YOUNG LADY** ...

and her miniature friend with the **BEAUTIFUL HAIR** ...

What's your point, old-timer?

The jerky is right!
It **DOES** make sense.
You just don't have all the
pieces of the puzzle yet!

THEN GIVE US THE PIECES!

Have faith,
Señorita
Gristlewurst.

Perhaps this
story isn't as
strange as
you think.

· CHAPTER 3 ·
THIS GAME IS FIRE

He misled us!
That one with all the
ears made this sound

EASY!

This isn't easy!

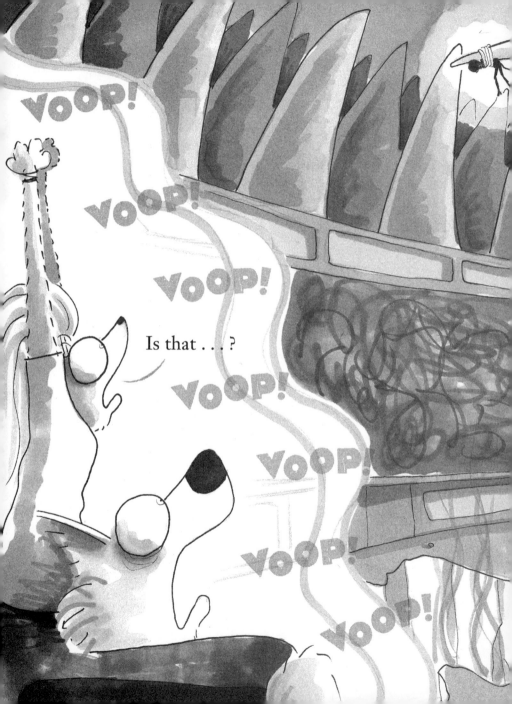

• CHAPTER 4 •
HERE COMES THE BUTT (SORRY... HAND)

So . . .
when we get there . . .
you and Zee and Milt will just . . . what?
Climb out of the ship and join The One?

Somethin' like that . . .

KA-
BLOW!

KA-BLOAW!

But what does that **LOOK LIKE?** You turn into a creature that looks part **DINOSAUR,** part **ALLIGATOR,** part **MULLET?**

Nah. It's more **SUBTLE** than that . . .

FA-ZOOOM!

· CHAPTER 5 ·
REGRETS
(HE HAS A FEW)

I'm not gonna lie, Foxy. My patience with these guys is running **OUT** ...

TURN UP THE HEAT! TURN UP THE HEAT! TURN UP THE HEAT! TURN UP THE HEAT! TURN UP THE HEAT! TURN UP THE HEAT! TURN UP THE HEAT! TURN UP THE

CRACK!

TURN UP THE HEAT!

She's going to fall!

Well, she might, Buddy, OR you could all **JUST GIVE UP** and I could use **MY LIMITLESS** POWER to save her.

You have a choice here.

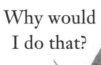

Why would
I do that?

I put my own problems onto you. But they were MY problems.

YOU were always just a really good kid.

THAT'S why I know you won't let us get hurt.

· CHAPTER 6 ·
GOOD-BYE DEAR FRIEND

FA-ZOOOM!

No! Milt! I don't want you to be absorbed into someone else! You're my *best friend* . . .
Oh, my dear boy. Don't you worry. Everything will be OK . . .
Sorry to ask, but you have **NO MEMORY OF ANYTHING.** How do you know it's going to be OK?

It's difficult to explain, **JOY**.
I can just feel it will be.

Whoa! Easy with
the "Joy" there, Buddy . . .

Oh, nonsense.
JOY is who you are.
Soon you will
understand that, too.

Wait . . . where'd she go?!

Huh?

It's time . . .

Set me down.

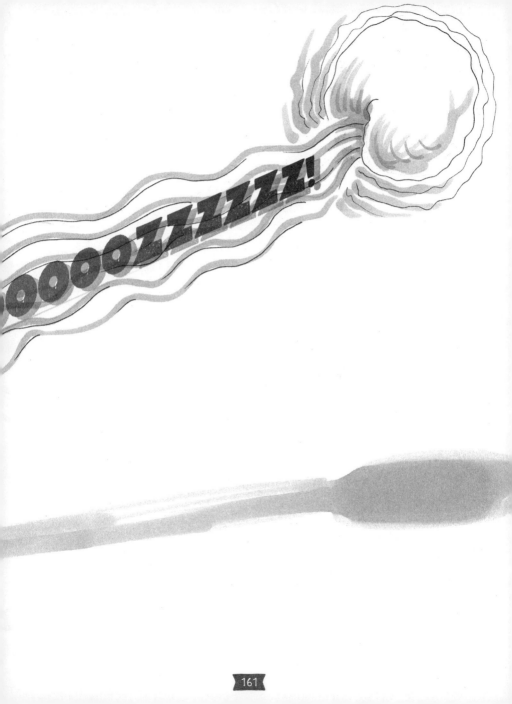

They missed.

THEY MISSED!

MASTER?!

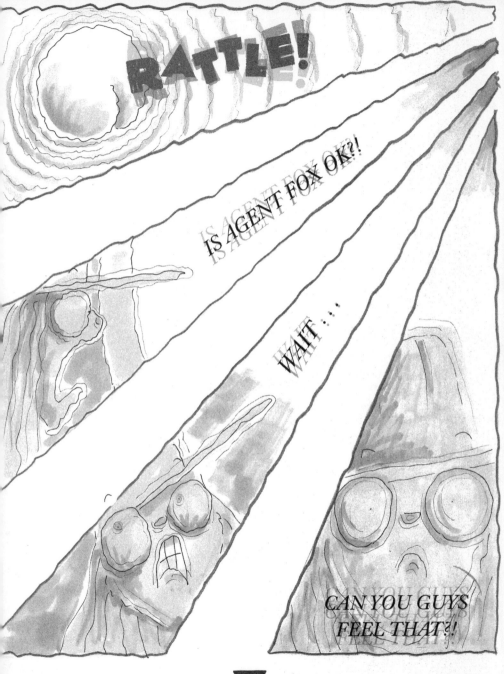

No.

She's not.

the BAD GUYS BOOK 18
COMING SOON . . .